DISTORTED LENS

ROY MERCHANT

First Printed in United Kingdom in 2021

Published by Relentless Realities Publishing

www.relentless-realities.com

Edited by: Charles Phillips and Christopher Walker

ISBN: 978-1-9168711-0-6

CONTENTS

DEDICATION

I dedicate this book to my wife Sue, who has shared with me this journey for a long-time. We have worked together to develop the next generation of positive, ambitious and loving people.

I also dedicate it to my children Adrian, Ainsley and Sophie and my grandchildren Kyle and Kanicia. They are our life's work, the primary reason we came to this planet.

I also dedicate it to everyone worldwide who are battling COVID-19. Nature will find a way, it always does. Be positive.

ACKNOWLEDGEMENTS

I Would like to thank the editors who worked on this for me to get it out error-free. In the end, I could not see a missing comma, full stop, or hyphen if it came up and slapped me in the face. Thanks to Roy Edwards, Charles Phillips and Christopher Walker for the job they did in helping to turn it from a lump of stone to something I am very proud of.

Big thank you to my reading group, who sat through my readings and gave me insights and inspirational thoughts when I needed them.

CHAPTER

ONE

2017

BY THE TIME I WAS ten, my mother had distorted the lens through which I viewed my father. In my earliest recollections of her describing him, she always spoke of what he did not do, what he could not do, and never what he did. He was the bogeyman on whom I built all my fears and misapprehensions. He was always going to disappoint me. Or so I thought. Why did she do that?

I could understand, perhaps, if this had happened–like some couples I have observed–towards the end of their relationship, when the consequences of their mistakes had caught up with them and they were more enemies than friends. In those circumstances, they might see each other in such a negative way, but as I said, my mother did this from the time I was born.

Was she programmed to do this? Was it her way of grooming her children, always to be on her side, always to be thinking of her, ensuring that her cup of love was always full? Or did she just hate my dad?

If it was hate, then why did she go through the entire business of having children with someone who disappointed her? Someone she had devalued and undermine while ensuring that their children would always see the lesser side of him. Why would she do that? How could she take away from her children another light in dark places, another voice to confirm the truth, another fountain of undying love?

All this came to mind as I sat at the corner table in the deli-cum- café, waiting for my father to arrive. He was always punctual, so I, too, always turned up in good time. My being there early would make him wonder if he was late when he saw me sitting in my chair there, totally relaxed. To my father, punctuality was essential. It was imperative to be on time or even five minutes early; he was forever saying.

We met for coffee the first Sunday of every month at the same café and always in the morning after he had gone to church and was on his way home. He came for coffee, but never touched the stuff, preferring to drink hot chocolate and eat a bowl of Amaretti biscuits, the round half globular disc ones, about an inch in diameter made from almond-based biscuit filled with Amaretto liqueur. He would just keep filling his mouth until the bowl was empty. On longer than usual meetups he would have three bowls of these biscuits.

He was dapper. He always dressed to impress. A long full-length cashmere double-breasted coat in black, matching the black cashmere hat, silk scarf folded as a cravat. The shoes were polished over delicate woollen socks, dark grey stripes emanating from black trousers with razor-sharp seams. I smiled at him, and for a moment, felt proud that in so many ways, I was exactly like him. Not what mother would have wanted, but it was true.

He unbuttoned his coat, then parted it with his hands from behind and sat down, his bottom on the chair and his coat overhanging onto the floor.

He was tall, slim built, and the wiry frame that had been his hallmark throughout his life was still present. Muscles not showing off, just there, somehow telling you in the subtlest of ways that he was not a man to be trifled with.

He smiled, and perfectly formed teeth were visible between his thin lips. His smile warmed up the room.

"So, how are things, son?" he said, gazing at me.

"I am good, Dad," I replied.

We spoke in staccato bursts, each hurrying to fill the gaps, making sure those horrible pauses, which showed tension, were not too apparent in our conversations.

I was twenty-nine years old, six years out of King's College London, five years at Price Waterhouse and clambering my way up the slippery pole of career advancement, relentlessly.

In those six years, I have got my first flat and invested

some of my earnings in shares which I think will do well in the next twenty years, if capitalism is still around. I now rent the flat out and have just purchased a detached home in an easy-to-look-at part of East London on the way to Epping on the A11.

In my imagination, I fight with the rabbits most mornings, before I go to work, to see who is master of the terrain. The rabbits normally win. They kind of stop, turn around, and give me the most contemptuous stare imaginable. If they were humans, they would frighten me. I smile as I turn the key and make my way to the underground station, leaving the rabbits to their devices.

This is where I plan to live at the moment. Five minutes' walk to the Central Line station, near local shops, supermarkets, and the swanky restaurants of South Woodford, Buckhurst Hill, and Loughton all within a ten-minute drive. This is as comfortable as I can imagine it, in this part of the world.

I intend to buy a couple more houses in this, the more salubrious part of West Essex, and rent them out to guarantee my early retirement. Going to do other things apart from working, by the time I am forty-five. Want to spend most of my adult life sharing the rewards for my hard work with my family. Do not have one yet, but that will come. Going to do all the heavy lifting now, so I do not have to, later. A bit like my dad.

Mother made it her duty to let us know how Dad had let her and us down again. It was so often done that in the end; we viewed our father through our mother's eyes.

He was the demon we had to endure. Why? It was never explained, but if we were all patient, then we would get through the ordeal.

She forced us to believe those things. The tribulation we could never see, but if Mum said there was a trial, then there must be one. After all, she is our mum, and she would never tell us anything that was not true, would she?

She was never happy about anything he did. It was as if she had married the wrong man, or the right man had not come along, or had turned up but not been spotted until a few days after she had given up on finding him and settled for what she had rather than what she wanted. That's how it felt to me at ten years old. Looking on and listening to my mum.

What she thought she was getting was some fantasy, a dream. The thing about fantasies is that they can never be wrong. People trapped in illusions never want to deal with realities, never need to compromise, grit their teeth and carry on, knowing *that* was the best outcome from the situation.

The imaginings were always going to win because you would never measure their consequence. Never compare them to anything real. The dream would forever remain in some cornfield where the sun is still shining, and two lovers are running towards each other in slow motion. There is never any mud, no flies and no mosquitoes to bite you back into the nightmare of life.

And when reality calls and demands its dues, those people will either collapse or run away. My mother ran.

In castigating my dad for everything, she somehow made

us kids feel our father was pointless, not made of anything worth taking seriously. Yeah, sure, we moved fast when he bellowed, but that was more in fear of his physical wrath, rather than being the only concern that would motivate us to be good–that fear of losing him. We were never afraid of that. By the time Mum's messages became a part of our psyche, we would not have cared too much if he was not around. I cringe when I remember this.

I often wondered why my mother never worked. Even when we kids were both in school and the excuse that the children needed her all day had evaporated, she still refused to go out and get even a part-time job. She preferred to tell us that Dad did not earn enough money to look after his family well and that's why we could only have the two holidays a year, unlike the Hutchison's, three doors away who had three or four. In her universe, despite her elite university degree, her job was to look after the house and keep the garden tidy and have long teatime sessions with her friends after her lunchtime jogging session. Everything else was down to Dad.

He had no chance of winning. I could see that now. I can reach out to him a little more these days, as I head towards adulthood and realise that compared to men, women think differently about most things. I also understand that his silence and her constant belittling of him were not a sign of his guilt. His muteness was only ever a sign of his absence.

Only now, do I understand that because she was a girl, my sister could get around the mythology that our mother wove around dad. She saw the real man, even at such a young age.

Rather than shun him and avoid the tough conversations, she nurtured their relationship and became very close to him, without ever disenfranchising mum in those early days. That showed a level of emotional maturity, which was fantastic for one so young. Me, I just avoided the conversations and would not talk to dad much when mum was around. He sensed that and thought I had no feelings for him, so even when mum was absent, our conversations were subdued.

Then she was gone. She just upped and left. One morning mum dropped us off at school, and that is the last time we saw her.

Ever.

CHAPTER
TWO

I PEERED AT HIM OVER the now half-empty cup of Jamaican Blue Mountain coffee I had ordered. For the first time, I had an insight into the strains he must have endured, never, ever giving out any sign that he knew how disparagingly mum spoke about him to us all those years ago.

I was his firstborn, the one born when all things were possible, and the future would unfold as he intended. There were no ambiguities, no maybes, no pushbacks that were ever going to restrain his enthusiasm. His confidence was so full. It was bubbling around the brim. He had all the answers, even to questions that had not yet been asked. Whatever it took to succeed, he would find it.

He was born in Hackney, a survivor from the old Mothers' Hospital on Lower Clapton Road, in Clapton.

His mother had escaped from Glendalough, a small town in County Wicklow, Ireland, famous only as a medieval place of worship founded by St. Kevin in the sixth century A.D. It was visited by Catholics and people of other religious faiths, from the United States as part of the "back to my roots", pilgrimage the Irish Americans love so much.

She left County Wicklow to come to England because she could not breathe in Ireland. Her enforced faith was like a rope around her neck, strangling her. All she was leaving behind was water and trees, interspersed every mile or so with a small cottage or religious buildings.

To her, 1959 London was raucous. There was music everywhere. It must have felt like there were no restrictions, and people could do what they wanted. There were grey days in the winter, but in the summer, everyone would go to the fetes and get-togethers in the parks around Hackney. It was there, in poverty-stricken and war-damaged East London, that she met my grandfather.

They met on Newick Road, Lower Clapton, when she was looking for a room to rent and had gone there to view one. The minute she opened her mouth, the lady who came to the door said, "Can't you read? No Irish, no Blacks, and no dogs," and slammed the door in her face. She was just about to apologise for not seeing the sign, when a man behind her said, "I guess she would have slammed it in my face as well." She turned around, looked at him and instead of crying, burst out laughing.

My grandfather had arrived from New Amsterdam, a small town in British Guiana, some three months before and, although a qualified accountant, could not get a job even as a bookkeeper. In frustration, he had taken the only position offered to him and was now running up and down the 106 bus saying "Fares, please" and spinning his ticket machine so fast he was becoming a legend on the buses. He always said, if he was going to be a bus conductor, then he was going to be the "best dyam conductor" in London.

With a job in hand, he was looking to move out of the room he shared on Powerscroft Road with the three guys from Demerara. He could no longer take the corned beef and rice they were living on and just wanted some space and some decent food. Anything and everything else could wait.

Grandmother, who I called Grandmum, always said that if it were not for her Catholic upbringing and a strong sense of rebellious independence, she would not have fallen in love with my father's dad. But fall in love with him, she did.

She used to tell me tales so sad that I often wondered why she shared them. She must have realised that they would leave a mark on me. That they would leave a stain on the way I viewed the world. But thinking about it, maybe that is precisely why she did it, so that I would never trust certain people, that I would always wonder what their motives were when they got too close to me.

The trouble is I could never be sure who I should not trust and the basis for their untrustworthiness. And my grandmother never ever spelled it out, just left it all full of ambiguity.

Who was I not supposed to trust? White people? My mother was white and my grandmother was also white. In fact, more than half of my relatives in England are white, so who am I supposed to trust. Was it *English* white people? If so, that means I should not trust my mother and all of her family. The only people she had decided I could trust were people from Guyana. My world was a lot bigger than that, and I had to trust other people or die from suffocation or claustrophobia.

She told me of her falling in love with my granddad within a month of meeting him on Newick Road in London. How after failing to see the house, they had jumped on the 106 bus and gone for a Wimpy and knickerbocker glory in Mare Street and just kept talking and laughing, oblivious of the unfriendly looks coming from some of the other customers in the Wimpy Bar. By the time they had said goodnight to each other, they had agreed to meet the next day to see *South Pacific* at the cinema. They also agreed to start looking for two rooms in the same house, anywhere in Lower Clapton. This they found in Mildenhall Road, the long street by the public toilets, just where the old 208 bus turned off the main road to park up by the pond.

The landlord was an old Jewish man who had suffered the same hate-filled venom from some people before the war and had reminded her that in those days, the sign used to say, "No Irish, no Jews and no dogs". He said in a joke that the Irish and the poor dogs had been on the list a long-time and it was good to see that the Jews were no longer on it and the blacks could have their turn, while the Jews had some rest.

They moved in and at first pretended that they were just acquaintances, (knew each other from the bus), but it did not take the other ladies in the house long to figure out what was going on.

Grandmum used to sit on that old chair reminiscing about 1959, always saying how it was the best year of her life, ever. How Granddad was like a life force, how he never stopped working. How they used to go for long walks in June and July and how July was the hottest month she had ever lived through. The temperature went as high as 90 degrees in some parts of London, and all the parks were full of people just enjoying themselves and fighting for some breeze.

She had left Glendalough, a young innocent, prim and proper Catholic girl in the spring of 1959 and there she was at the end of June 1960, pushing her Pedigree pram down Mare Street to register her two-week old baby at the Town Hall. Dad was born on Thursday, 16th June 1960.

She said once, in another moment of subdued anger, with the tears running down her cheeks and the laughter mingling with the sniffs, as she fought her way out of that negative place to which her mind and memories had gone, about how the lady behind the counter registering the babies, had long chats with the mothers of the other newborn and cooed at them as she took down details of their birth. She looked as if she would love to be the mother of those children.

But when it was Grandmum's turn, the mood changed as the registrar glimpsed the baby in the pram and saw he was not a white baby, but was much darker than what she was used to. In her confusion, she became angry, and her attitude changed. She looked down at Grandmum and had no interest in cooing at the baby. The atmosphere became cool, and the dealings matter-of-fact.

As Grandmum left the room, she looked back only to see the registrar ushering other ladies from other offices into the room and pointing at her, shaking her head as if someone had committed a great evil or died.

Grandmum realised that the hate she endured when going out with Granddad was something that was going to be passed on to her children. She felt as if the entire world would never be innocent again.

Granddad died in 1992 in his beloved Berbice. He only went back to tidy up his mum and dad's grave and look after the land, pay some tax and come back.

We had agreed he would take me to see Robin Williams in the film *Hook* on his return. He died of a heart attack in the house on Republic Road and Grandmum and Dad brought him back to be buried in Manor Park Cemetery.

Grandmum lasted another four years resenting Granddad every day for leaving her behind. I heard her say many times that if she had known he was going to leave her alone so young, in her early fifties, she would never have married him.

Her grieving was sullen, filled with regrets, resentments, and paranoia. She ended up isolating her other two children (my distant aunt and uncle, who I just do not see), and in the end, only my dad had the patience to love her unconditionally.

Dad became certain that being mixed-race made his life

impossible. He felt that all white people (one half of him) would reject him, the way Grandmum's family had rejected her. We never met her half of the family, who had cut her off when they found out that she was having a baby with a so-called coloured man.

She had told me, when I was the ripe old age of six, how she had gone over to Glendalough at Christmas in 1959, three months pregnant and naïve enough to think that her family did not have a bad thought in their minds about coloured people. They were not like the English and would welcome the new baby when it arrived.

Her father went into a rage, an incandescent fury when she took the black-and-white picture out and showed him the baby's father. He had said to her that even at three months pregnant; she had to go back to England and get an abortion. Otherwise, she would not set foot back in that house. She then turned to her mother for support, but all she got was a hard slap in her face, after which her mum picked up the unopened bags and threw them out of the door. She never went back to Ireland, and Granddad was the only family she could count on after that.

In those four years after Granddad's death, she lived with us on the weekends and gave me a jaundiced view of everything. She died in the summer of 1996, and we placed her on top of Granddad in Manor Park Cemetery. I often wondered whether he would have appreciated being buried with the woman she had become.

"What you doing later? Wanna catch a film down at Lee

Valley?" Dad's quiet voice brought me back from the memories I was revisiting.

"You not in a hurry today, Dad?" I asked, wondering if I should find an excuse to avoid the film and go back home.

"No, I have got some time, besides we have not seen a film together for a long, long time."

Going to the cinema brought back memories of those days when we used to go to the pictures every Saturday afternoon. We must have seen every Disney film that was ever made. My favourite, of course, was *The Lion King*. I loved Rafiki; he was like a mystic warrior. We must have seen that film at least ten times.

I smiled as I remembered those days. I did not remember Mum coming more than a few times, though. She hated movies, preferring to go out shopping with her friends, while Dad, Sis and I went out all day. We would start out at a museum down Kensington, District and Central line back to Leytonstone, picked up the car, in for a quick McDonalds, then down to Lee Valley Odeon, or UCI as it was called then, for the main event, a movie.

We loved the movies, especially cartoons, adventures, science, fictions, everything. Dad and I must have seen every under-12 film that ever came out between 1992 and 1998. Sis started coming in July 1998 and stayed right until she and I started getting embarrassed about going to the cinema with our dad.

Even though Mum had the complete day to herself, somehow she would find ways of complaining about our day, the day in which she had taken no part. She always had to sour our time and make us feel bad. She had to make us find something to be annoyed with Dad about. And Dad, in his innocence, saw nothing, felt nothing, heard nothing. In his universe, everything was right and dandy. In ours, the issues were stacking up like dominoes, and one day my sister and I knew the dominoes would fall.

"Come on then Dad, let's catch that film," I said as we left the café and headed towards the car that would take us down the A406 to The Lee Valley Odeon.

CHAPTER
THREE

I FIRST NOTICED THAT MY mother differed from me when I was four years old. It wasn't the colour of her skin that gave it away. While our skin tones were different, hers a full cream and mine café au lait, or milk with a hint of coffee, that difference was not significant enough for me to notice at that age. No, it was her eyes that gave it away. I did not know the exact colour. I only knew the colours blue, red, yellow, white and black. Everything else was just words that had no meaning to me at all.

Her eyes had the colour and sparkle of a finely cut and polished piece of aquamarine gemstone compared to mine, which was the colour of hazelnut. Her irises were somewhere between blue and green depending on the light or whether she was squinting. Most of all, I remember her smile.

Mother had the most elegant of smiles. The smile radiated from within her, and although it was not a constant feature of her face, when it appeared, it had a beauty that filled the room with radiance. In one of her dark moods, though, her eyes took on a dark blue colour. It was when she was in one of those moods that I first noticed her eyes.

I noticed that when she had dark blue eyes; she kept saying the same things about Dad: he was never at home; he expected her to do everything, he never had time to take me to the nursery. "No time at weekends to take the lad out so that I could rest," she would mutter. She was not saying it to anyone in particular, but she was not trying to make sure I did not hear her.

I remember thinking to myself, "Bad Daddy", but that would disappear the moment he came home and picked me up and ran around the living room, with me on his shoulders. I would duck down so that I did not bang my head on the ceiling. I kept laughing, in fits and starts, until I sounded like a donkey braying. When I looked at Mum, her eyes were still dark blue, and she would ignore me for hours after that. Eventually, I became apprehensive about playing with Dad when she was around. In the end, I just became afraid of playing with Dad all the time, in case I got "punished".

My little sister came along when I was five years old, in January 1993. I wonder if they conceived her as a distraction to Grandmum, who lived with us at weekends. My grandmum did everything to ensure that her bereavement darkened the environment in which we all lived. Mum struggled with Grandmum, and sometimes you could almost see the painted smile crack, the façade of politeness wearing so thin, you wondered whether she would explode.

In her bereavement, Grandmum became a negative force, and after she started living with us half the week, she brought with her all the anger, frustration, and disappointment she felt at a life endured, a disappointment compared to the life she thought might have been hers had she not gone to Newick Road that day in 1959 and met Granddad.

The tension generated by Mum and Grandmum was like a living being. It permeated the environment. Slowly at first. Words said, not responded to, followed by silence. An hour later a response might come, but it would be cold, edgy, lips pursed, closed, like a sliver, a thin line on a pumpkin. Further silence, a door slammed as a person went out, followed by a banging of the bathroom door and threatening mutterings.

The atmosphere grew colder and colder until it evolved into a life force of its own. Once alive, it did everything to stay blooming. As it grew, it got so thick you could almost cut it with a knife. It became so vast; it took over the house and only left when Grandmum died.

When the negative environment was grown and Grandmum was in the nadir of her grief, she could see nothing good in anyone. She would have welcomed death just to be with her beloved. When all she had left to live for was the certainty of her own demise, she would attack Mum with her negativity, which was said in a near-silent, almost viper-like hiss. One time I heard her say to my mum,

"Sometimes I feel my son was a trophy to you, another notch on your bedpost of self-righteousness, an almost meaningless gesture about you, not him.

"Did you, no, do you love him? Or was he a certificate you could take home to Mum and Dad to show how you had evolved? How different you were from them, how you were now a multiculturalist, a hip, with-it member of the London diverse elite.

"Was your smile victorious when you saw the look of consternation and confusion on your father's face as he saw the photograph of my son that you were sharing with him?

"Did you laugh at them, as I did with my own parents so long ago, as they tried to tell you of the difficulties you would face?

"You must have said to yourself, 'What do these old farts or fogies know? This is now. They are living in the past.

"Do you realise now that some things do not change? That fear turns to hatred, and when hate is in the room, it is hard for love to find any light or even space?

"As for my son, he should have known better. After all, he saw growing up. After all, we told him.

"He must love you so much that he was prepared to put up with all this bitterness you wear on your sleeves."

Then she stormed into the garden to sit under the damson tree, shaking her head to push the unwanted thoughts away from her mind.

It was easier after Sis was born. Mum had something to occupy her with, and although she and Grandmum competed for Sis's love, Mum got enough of it to feel satiated. Dad and I did not get a look in.

I was coming up six years of age when I realised that my mother also felt the difference between her and me. Six when I knew that my mother was ashamed of me.

I had heard the word 'coon' in the playground but did not think anyone was referring to me, even at five it felt like it was a nasty way of talking about those Africans who spoke with the funny accent, that no one else in the schoolyard understood.

Mum had collected me from school and with Sis, still newborn and bundled up in baby clothes, with only her face showing in the baby carrier and asleep, we made our way out of the school playground and headed down the High Road, past the church. Past the Gates car showroom, turning left into George Lane and down the hill towards her favourite coffee shop.

She was holding the pram and my right hand with her left hand, keeping me on the inside away from the traffic and also using both hands to steer Sis's pram.

As she went past, this old woman in a white coat, with white hair and blue eyes, looked at her and said "bloody coon lover". This caused my mother to let go of my hand and started walking faster and faster away from me, practically as if she was running away.

I did not know what was happening, so I started

scampering after her, and the faster I ran, the more rapidly she went away from me, until I screamed, "Mum, wait for me!". That seemed to penetrate the nightmare she was enduring and brought her back to her senses and into my world. She stopped and hugged me and squeezed me, then kissed my cheek with her freezing lips, and as she did, I saw the tears running down her face from her especially dark blue eyes.

Nothing in my mother's young life had prepared her for the background noise of disapproval, the looks of abhorrence and alienation she would face the minute she declared she was in love with someone who was not English or entirely white.

It may have been OK, had he been French, maybe German and at worst Italian, Spanish or Portuguese, but not the son of an Irish woman and someone from the West Indies whose ancestors were slaves. Her father felt humiliated in his quiet way. He was disappointed that after a thousand years of keeping his bloodline the same as "William the Conqueror", or was it Anglo-Saxon? He struggled to remember the hand-me-down tales from his grandfather about which side they fought on in the Battle of Hastings, but at least he knew his ancestors were there. His only daughter had let the family down by going off and falling in love with some Johnny Foreigner with dark skin. That Dad was born in London had escaped him.

"She did nothing by half, always had to go the whole way. She couldn't have just had a dilly dally with him, a sneaky taste of forbidden fruit when no one was looking, and erase it from her memory the way we used to do. Oh no, she had to get involved and bring home something that no one wanted," he thought.

He tried his hardest to get her to see sense in his subtle way, but she knew her father too well and had an answer for all the logical, but silly, arguments he put forward. All the points about being ostracised were things she had never experienced before and could not envision them happening in England when they met in the autumn of 1980. He was an old twenty-year-old, and she was a young eighteen-, coming up nineteen-year-old.

The world she knew was full of people falling in love with others from outside of their tribes and comfort zone. Even some of her Asian acquaintances were marrying whites, blacks and mixed-race people all over London.

My Mum had always lived in polite circles, where the actual feelings lived below the surface, where the dagger went in when no one was looking. She did not even know that there were any daggers around.

If my dad had not been so in love with Mum and her *joie de vivre*, he might have been able to warn her to take it slow, to check out the lay of the land before making any commitments. But he was smitten, so in love with the aquamarine-eyed girl who laughed like it was the only thing left to do. Who only ever saw the goodness in people, who never had a bitter bone in her entire body, that he forgot his journey so far in this, his homeland and started believing her version of his reality.

Her natural exuberance allowed him to think that maybe, just maybe, he had misinterpreted the slights, the fears, the cold lack of engagement he had felt as he tried to integrate and grow up in the society of his birth.

She made him feel clean, like everything was possible. Like racism was just something to be laughed at and ignored until it crawled back under the stone of fear whence it came. Together they would change those negative thoughts and create a better world. Or so he thought.

I watched, unable to change a single thing for the better, as the light in her eyes became dimmer. Hearing the confidence in her voice becoming fainter as the negative body language and looks of disgust from those around her changed her. She felt ashamed of the people she knew and once loved, and started wondering if she was in the wrong.

By the time Sis came along, all the vivacity and *Élan* that shone through those aquamarine eyes had gone and replaced by negativity and raw suspicion, the hopelessness, the frustrated anger that life had the temerity to prove her wrong. All she had left was the ability to find faults in everything.

She found faults in the way Dad spoke, the way he would laugh, that half faltering, hiccupping kind of laugh. Almost primordial, it would remind me of a deep bass drum, telling me and anyone who wanted to hear that he was alive, he was here, and he did not care who knew it.

She would find negative things to say about him in front of her white friends, almost as if it was essential for her to join in the mickey-taking, but Mum was never, ever on his side. There was always some slight, some dig about his hair, the shape of his nose, the length of his fingers. Even when the comment could have been positive, she chose not to make it so. And she often complained about things he could do nothing about.

One day I looked at my dad and for the first time recognised that I was the spitting image of him. It was then that I wondered if my mother felt the same about me as she did about Dad.

But Mum was Mum. She was the rock upon which I had built all my faith in humanity. My closeness to her overrode everything. When I was with her, I felt no fear, no uncertainties, no restrictions. Her instructions I had to follow, her likes and dislikes I had to support and to reflect on how I saw the world. Between the ages of six and ten, I saw everything from the perspective my mother had forced upon me. And I soon paid the price for that.

CHAPTER

FOUR

I TOOK A SIDEWAYS GLANCE at my dad as we came out of the cinema, and I smiled. I was twenty-nine, and still in awe of him; somewhere in the recesses of my psyche, I wanted to please him, to get him to say "well done" to me. It came to me he has always cared for me and that I was not alone. I always wanted my dad to love me.

The film we saw was a lousy version of the Superman and Batman franchise. Like a lot of things these days, it promised a lot but delivered very little. "Waste of twenty pounds", I thought as we got back into the car and headed out of the carpark, turned right at the lights heading towards Ponders End, then Woodford via the back doubles of North Chingford and Woodford Green.

I was about to drop him back to South Woodford when I felt alone and just wanted to extend the afternoon into the evening to spend a little more time with him.

"Fancy a chat, Dad? Long-time since we had a good chat. Remember when we used to sit down in the garden and talk about Granddad and his childhood in Berbice and you all in Hackney, back in the day? Miss those chats, Dad. Funny, you know, when I was a kid, I used to want to run away from those chats. It is only now I realise how enthralled I was with the conversations, because they were so rare."

"I don't mind. Let's go by you. Haven't been to your place for a little while."

"That's good. I'll just stop by that restaurant down by the station and get a takeaway."

We got a Chinese takeaway and went back to my place. I put the cartons in the oven to warm up some more (Dad never liked cold food), opened a bottle of white wine and asked Dad what Grandmum and Granddad were like when he was a kid.

He looked at me as if I had never asked him that question before, and I recalled that he just did not get around to talking about them much these days.

We knew everything about Mum's side of the family because in their absence and with us never meeting them in person, Mum told us everything about them, and you could see she missed them.

Her sadness about not being in contact with them was like a nagging toothache. It was always there, reminding us that things were not perfect. Something else to put right. The loss was never-ending.

Because of this, she regularly spoke about the memories she had of her Aunt Maggie, Uncle Archibald and his growing senility, her Dad's hair falling out and him buying a toupee. But the hairpiece he bought was not the right colour, and every time he went to the pub, people would nudge each other and laugh at him behind his back. She would recall how he started wearing a hat when he found out that they were laughing at him, and then one day the hat and the toupee fell off his head on a day trip to Worthing.

My Mum used to be in fits of laughter as the memories from her childhood came flooding back and she saw her Dad running after the hat and the toupee with the whole family laughing at him as every time he got close to the hat, the wind would tease him and push it closer to the sea.

By the time he picked the hat out of the sea and turned around, the wig was also in the sea, limp and looking like an old piece of rag.

Seeing the funny side of it, he put them both on his head and walked around with the limp hat and wig all afternoon, getting the weirdest of looks from everyone on Worthing Beach.

Like I say, we knew everything about Mum's family, though we had never met them. Up to the time she bolted, she spoke about them and made them real. We understood how it worked, the rhythms and patterns of all the individuals, but because Dad did not seem to have any space to tell his story, his myths and legends never got discussed. We knew almost nothing about that half of us. At twenty-nine, I felt like half a person. Like one side of me was incomplete.

"What do you want to know, son?"

"Tell me everything, Dad."

"I thought I had told you and your sister all there was to know, Sunshine, but like a lot of things in my life, I realise that sometimes people just say 'yes' to stop you talking so that they can get on with what they are doing, or they were not interested.

"I have been thinking about writing a book about my life up to now and have started in the early years, up to when our lives changed forever. I will email it to you when I get home. Have a read and let me know what you think. It is an early draft so don't edit it for me and point out the spelling errors. I will get to that much further down the line. You can let me know how it feels and whether I should tell the story."

"Oh brilliant, I will read it as soon as you send it," I said.

While he was talking he took off his long coat, folded it in half with the sleeves hidden inside and touching each other, looked around for somewhere to put it and put it on the double settee in the living room where it had the seats all to itself. He then sat almost upright in the single leather chair with a view of the garden, arms straight out and resting on each knee. He took a sip of the hot chocolate and said:

"I am proud of you and Sis, you know, son, always has been, always will be. I feel you two are my masterpieces. Now, where is this food you promised?"

We ate while talking about nothing in particular for a couple of hours then I dropped him back home and waved goodbye to him and the nosey neighbour next door, and came home, planning to have an early night to catch up on some sleep I had been missing out on lately.

I came back home, went to my laptop and saw an email with attachments from Dad. I opened the email, then the attachment and started reading and this is what my Dad said to me:

Hi Sunshine,

Here is where I am up to in that first draft I was talking about. Haven't got a title for it yet, but it will come.

Sometimes, I feel like my life has just been a series of happenstances, you know, son. Many coincidences that have shaped how I view the world. Some have been fantastic, and some have put me in situations that I did not want to be in. I have survived them all and am here right now, talking to you. And I am so pleased about that.

The book starts on the next page.

PROLOGUE

TO MY BELOVED CHILDREN. I have spoken to you both on so many occasions about me, Mum, and what happened when she left in 1998. But I do not know if it is because you don't want to talk about it, or whether you are fed up with the whole thing, but I never get the sense that you have integrated it into reality. I am writing this so that you know who I am and what happened from my perspective.

I am penning it as a letter to you both and it covers the first part of my life. It is a bit like the first act of a long play or story. Life, though, has to be taken overall to see how it ends up.

It starts with me thinking about my own parents and finishes with your mum leaving us.

I am writing it to both of you because it is me, having a chat with you two.

Do you know, my mum and dad never disagreed with each other, or if they did, I never saw it or heard it. Never. They reserved any bitterness they might have felt for the people who took it on themselves to make their lives hell. The lady at the nursery who held my arm like it was something dirty that had to be put down as soon as possible whenever Mum dropped me off. The garage mechanic who put grease all over the front passenger seat when he realised that my father, a black man, owned a fancy car.

By the time I had enough sense to know anything about jobs and work, Dad had traded in his conductor's uniform and was going to work in a suit as a bookkeeper at 55 Broadway, the London Transport Head Office.

Every morning Mam would pack his sandwiches and flask of tea, and he would get the bus to Liverpool Street, where he would get on the tube to St. James's Park and walk to 55 Broadway. Wearing the suit was all he had to show for the effort he had put in to get his accountant's qualification in Georgetown all those years ago.

He would smile as he recalled all the effort he and Mum had put in. I was now about six, and we had moved from the room in Powerscroft Road into a flat in Rushmore Road, just past the school. They were also saving every penny they could find to buy a house.

1966 was a glorious year. England won the World Cup in July. I was six years old, and for the first time, I felt at home. All everyone would talk about was the fact that we, I say we (which included me, the milky coffee-coloured boy with the light brown eyes and frizzy hair) had won the World Cup, beating West Germany.

I did not know what the relationship was between England and Germany at that age. The understanding would come in an osmosis-like way over the years. It kinda crept up on you in every conversation about what it is to be British. It was practically as if all our history had been a blank page–and the only significant thing achieved by this state that ruled a quarter of the world was the fact that we had beaten Germany twice in wars and in the World Cup. Almost as if that solely described what it is to be British.

Dad said that it took him one and a half hours to get to work each day and the same to get back home. The job he had to do was below his skill grade–invoices to add up and expenses to pay.

They gave the very technical accountancy work to the people in the big office. Every now and again one of these so-called managers would go out into the bookkeepers' section, peer down at them over the top of his glasses, almost as if studying some creature from a subspecies, decide that there was no one to tell off and meander back to his office for a cigarette.

There were days when Dad would have traded in his suit for his old conductor's uniform to avoid being the only black man in a crowded room. The silence almost drove him to despair. No one spoke to him unless he talked to them first, and even then, the conversation took the tone of name, rank and official number only. As for talks outside the office, that was a definite no-no.

On a good day when he got to have a joke with someone in the office, the banter would stop, with everyone becoming strangers again the minute they put the coats on and made their way down to the exit. It was almost as if they did not work in the same office. The next morning when they got back in the office, away from the prying eyes of the outside world, the conversations could start again as if nothing had happened.

My sister came in the spring of 1967. By then I had been on my own–a single child–for so long that I never got used to being part of a family. In my mind, it was always just me, Mum, and Dad. The last of us, my young brother, came along in the winter of 1968 I was like a second dad to tiny sister and brother, and they stuck to each other like glue–leaving me out in the cold.

My siblings and I never bonded; I am sorry to say. It was almost as if they differed from me. They saw nothing the way I did. By the time they came along, people who had come from the Caribbean were creating a community. There were even nurseries being created where the black children were not alone.

In my nursery, I was always alone. I was always the only child with the light coffee-coloured skin, whose hair was being tousled by children and adults alike, as if I was some exotic dolly that fascinated everyone, but was unloved.

My brother and sister went to nurseries and a school that had a high number of children of mixed heritage, children whose parents came from the Caribbean and India, as well as the majority whose background was English and white.

They grew up being able to speak in a way that made them fit in with all the cultures, accents, and enunciations that were coming into being across London.

My experience of being the only "coloured" child in my

nursery and then my school and my clubs had driven me to develop a rather "proper" English accent, and try as I might, I could never lose it. I could never speak Guyanese English or even Irish English, without sounding ridiculous. And as for Jamaican patois, that was a definite no-no.

As we got older, the differences got more extreme, until we nearly stopped speaking to each other. They saw me as a snob, a wannabe white boy, a "Bounty" as I heard my sister mockingly call me one day. Someone ashamed of who they were. And all my protestations were too mild and not believed.

Mum was a proud woman, delighted with all the decisions she had made about love. She had no doubts about who the man in her life should be and defended him through thick and thin. Her abandonment by her parents was proof of her commitment. She was a fighter, extra-ordinary and more of a warrior for black rights than my father could ever be.

They had conditioned my father from the time he was born to always take the back seat, to accept second best and not to fight too hard for what he wanted in case they beat him up, spat at him–or even worse. His strategy was to wait until the white men grew bored with discrimination and went on to something else–allowing him his freedom, his time in the sunshine. Father's way was to use stealth and patience to get where he wanted to go, even if it took him and his kind a thousand years. Mother wanted equality sooner than that and was prepared to fight for it.

My younger siblings followed the path of my mother, and I thought the strategy my father used was the best way of negotiating my way through the culture England imposed on what it describes as foreigners. I integrated into the English way of life. I blended so well that I lost myself. And while my brother and sister were cheering on the marchers and fighting inequality with civil disobedience, poetry, and song, even at their early age, I would have gladly changed my name out of embarrassment. It is hard to go through these thoughts again.

I struggled with my identity. You know, I struggled. Could not tell my dad how painful the name-calling was to me. Dreaded going to school, to be called Coon, Wog, Jungle Bunny, Nignog, so I told him everything was fine, that if any boy called me names, I would beat them up. I was saying this, and those boys petrified me. They all seemed bigger than me, and everywhere I looked there was a sea of white faces, daring me to challenge the status quo, goading me to say something that they could use to justify their violence.

I would have been an excellent student, but being asked every day, I mean every day, if I ate the cat food Kitekat made me stop thinking about learning. All I wanted to do was get through the day, go home and lie to my mother, telling her all was well as I slunk up the stairs to my bedroom.

The "coloured" boys in the other schools were not to be messed with as they roamed the playground in packs (the white kids' words) and they would sort anyone caught messing about with any of them out after school. I longed for the time that I would have other "coloured" or non-white kids in my school, but it never came. I left as soon as I could at sixteen in the summer of 1976.

I became confused and did not know what I was going to do with my life. Getting angry and frustrated at everything and everyone. Still the "Bounty" looking down at everyone, laughing at the way my siblings spoke, but achieving nothing at all. They did not look to me for older brother's guidance. They got that from the older boys in their school, the other "black" kids at their club in Mare Street.

By now everyone is calling themselves black, even children from mixed relationships. Everyone but me. I am becoming invisible, and no one cares. At least that's what I thought.

One day in late 1976, I was sitting in front of the TV, trying to keep my head from exploding from all the unhealthy thoughts and negative energies that were close to overwhelming me, when Dad said, "I am going to see Mum in Guyana, wanna come?"

He made it sound like he was just popping across the road to have a quick chat with his mum, rather than travelling nearly five thousand miles to another country. I was so down that I said, "Yes, alright, Dad." And that's how my life changed. That's when I became the man I am today.

I realised later, much later, that Mum, Dad, and Granny had planned this so far behind my back that I was incapable of seeing it.

My granny was a dark, mahogany-coloured woman. She was the darkest person I had ever seen. I had never thought of my father as being very brown. In fact, I had never thought of my dad as being black. He was just Dad. I had no context to imagine him in. He was just my dad. I looked at my Granny and could see the stark similarity between my dad and her and then between her and me and I started getting to know who I was. Her hair was black and shiny, almost as if she had just washed it in coconut oil and had not bothered to dry it.

She was hugging Dad and smiling at me. Her smile was so engaging, so non-judgemental, so warm, that it forced my lips to part, my mistrust to depart–and a smile to appear on my face for the first time in a long while. She was about five foot five inches tall, with expressive brown eyes and a manner that made me feel at ease.

She had become a mother at nineteen, and although my grandparents wanted other children, try as they might, another one never came.

In 1976 Granny met us at the airport after the long flight from London to New York and then the Boeing 707 from New York to Timehri International Airport on the banks of the Demerara River, near Georgetown. She must have caught the look of trepidation, or was it disappointment, in my eye as Dad lifted her off the floor and spun her around and around, scream-ing "Mama, Mama, a soh glad fe see yu. It has been so long!"

It shocked me to be asked to assimilate this lady into my life, but I was more stunned to see dad holding someone other than Mum and speaking in a way I had never heard him talk before. It was virtually as if all the tensions of living in England was gone and he was himself again. No more pretence, no more lies. My father was home. Home at last.

My Granny kept looking at me and smiling all the way from the airport to New Amsterdam. She was analysing every section of me, from my head to my toes, and comparing me with all the other family members from her side and Grandpa's, who she could remember. Trying to see where I fitted in and whose bloodline was dominant. She caught my eyes and turned away in embarrassment, caught doing something she did not want anyone to see.

The taxi took four and a half hours to travel the ninety-five miles from the airport to Georgetown. From there it went on to Success, past Lusignan, Non-Pariel, Enmore, Clonbrook, Mahaica and all the other little one-horse towns, hamlets and villages down to the bridge at Rosignol then past Berbice High School. We stopped every half hour to quench our thirst and relieve ourselves as the mosquitoes feasted on our blood.

The driver sat there, avoiding the potholes with the skill of a fighter pilot and the dexterity of a professional juggler. He did all this as he chit-chatted all the way, never once looking at the road. He seemed to know every gulley and pothole on the road to New Amsterdam.

Dad and I got out of the car, looked at each other, and smiled. Granny and the taxi driver carried on as if the trip was just another day of ordinary life in Guyana. And indeed it was.

The house was on Republic Road, a quiet, tree-lined avenue that was once genteel a long time ago when New Amsterdam was the capital of Guyana. Now it was still one of the best roads in New Amsterdam, but it no longer shone. It was living on its past glory and hoping no one noticed.

The road, part of which is also called Winkle Road, starts at the same point as Main Street and follows behind it to Berbice High School, where it ends. From Granny's house, you could *look back down towards Smythfield and see The First Baptist Church and the Eden Seventh Day Adventist Church in one frame of a photograph.*

The house felt comfortable, old furniture standing proud, not making any noise, in case it got noticed and thrown out. Veranda polished until it gleamed, the red wax smelling all the way from the front gate. A white wood-framed house with glass windows and a zinc roof. Very upmarket Caribbean style, old world and outdated from where I am coming from. It all seemed so backward, so out-of-date compared to the brand-new houses that were being built in London.

We got in the house and Granny showed me to my room, a small space with a bed, a desk, and a lot of books. It had more books than I remember us having at home. Dad had forgotten who he was in England. These books told me he had come from a family of educated people who were interested in learning.

In England, he seemed to be so busy; he did not have time to read The Daily Mirror *or even* The Evening News, *let alone the books that were proudly displayed in this room.*

There was The Black Jacobins *by C. L. R. James, a rack of all Shakespeare's plays and sonnets, many books on accountancy, many of the works of Alain LeRoy Locke and W.E.B. Dubois and new books on the shelves by Walter Rodney and E.R. Braithwaite.*

It astounded me that the bookshelf of an old lady in the backwaters of Guyana contained books about the black experience that I had never heard of. And so, I started reading, and in the end, read every single one of them.

Dad and I went all over Guyana–well, the developed areas anyway–which are along the coast. We traversed some rivers. We swam in the Demerara, fished on the Berbice and went rafting on the Essequibo rivers from morning till night, and in those few weeks we were together, I got to know my Dad. He was a simple man living in a complex world, and although he was bright in the Caribbean, England overwhelmed him with its rules, its cultural differences, and its secrets.

In Guyana, he knew where he stood. If someone did not like him, it might be because of his height, being too smart or just because they did not like him. And if he wanted to, he could find a way of changing their minds for the better, be it through kindness, attention or even gifts.

In England, most of the times the smile does not mean what you think it means, he would often say. You just do not know where you stand, and that filled him with insecurity and made him a prisoner of his uncertainties.

It was when we were fishing on the banks of Berbice River between the Krishna temple and Sister's Post Office that Dad broke my heart. We were under the tree, sitting on some rock and trying to make sure that the sun on the stone did not fry our bottoms when Dad said to me:

"Your Mum and I think you should stay over here for a while, you know, son."

I laughed at the joke, saying "Yeah, hilarious, Dad", looking up–only to see that my Dad was not joking. He and Mum had planned this thing without telling me. Had dragged me all the way over to some godforsaken hole in South America to abandon me. Did Granny know of this as well? Did the three of them plan this behind my back?

Why would Mum dump her oldest son in one of the poorest countries in the world if she loved him? At that moment, when the truth hit me when I saw the tears well up in my father's eyes, I felt the loneliest I have ever felt in my life.

My father tried to explain, on that riverbank, under that enormous tree shading the deep blue river.

He said that he was not sure that England was ready for his children; that I was born when there were not enough black children in England to look after each other. That in trying to integrate, we were losing our souls, and while the younger ones had enough kids who looked like them to withstand some of the prejudice and hate that was part of our daily lives, he did not think I had a chance. He felt I needed to find out who I was before I could become who I should be.

He told me he had bought only one ticket back to England; that I was going to stay with Granny and enrol at the Berbice High School for a year to take my GCEs and we would see how things go after that.

Dad left the following day, and as Granny and I waved him off at the airport, I did not know that it would be nearly four years until we would meet again.

I did not cry. No one was ever going to see me cry. But Granny knew how I was feeling. As we stood there watching the most important connection I had with the only life I ever knew disappear through the departure lounge, she slowly touched my hand, rubbed it up and down and I allowed her to entwine her warm, soft fingers with mine. She gave my hand a gentle squeeze.

I will remember that squeeze for the rest of my life. It was a grasp that said, all will be OK, I know what to do, and I will look after you until you are ready for England. Or until England is ready for you.

Could not speak on the way back to the house on Republic Road, I stared out of the car window and started re-engineering my life, my plans and how I was going to get the better of this situation. It was there on that drive I realised that if I wanted to achieve anything; I had to do it on my own. Could trust no one. I had to make sure that I had a get-out plan for all eventualities that might befall me. And so, at sixteen years of age, I started becoming the man I am today.

Granny became my mother, someone who, in the end, understood me more than anyone else in my life. She knew I was proud, and she nourished that pride with a meticulous attitude toward cleanliness, tidiness, and precision.

She used to say: "The last thing you should do before you go out of the house is to look at yourself in the mirror. Make sure that everything is how you want it to be. The world is a hard and unforgiving place, so make sure you have nothing to be forgiven."

"You know you are going to be busy, so make sure that you do not need to be thinking if your shoes are clean enough, if your suit is ironed, or if your shirt has dirt on it. These daily chores just occupy valuable time and over the years take away from you months, if not years of wondering, when you could

be doing. Check as you leave the house and all should be fine." Granny said. My mother never told me that!

She would iron the shirts and then get me to iron the trousers. She would heat the iron on the wooden fire, damp a piece of an old sheet and use that to iron the pants–leaving no crease, apart from the one standing proud and running down the front and back of my school uniform trousers. I was the smartest young man in Berbice School. Nobody laughed at me.

All the other kids laughed with me until I understood the rhythms of the language, the jokes, the patter, the mickey-taking and all.

Everybody was equal. Nobody thought they were better than anybody else. Everybody thought they were brighter than others, but not better.

On those hot South American Caribbean nights, we used to sit on the veranda of that house on Republic Road and chat about Guyana's customs. We chatted about where the words came from. The ones came from India, the ones that came from West Africa, and the ones that were always here with the Arawaks and the Caribs.

On a Sunday, we would walk all over the town, Granny pointing out all the landmarks of New Amsterdam, the churches, and how long they had been there. Who lived in the place where the Dutch landed when they arrived in the first place? We would walk all the way from the schoolhouse down to the main street, go down by the stream, sit under the tree, she ended up telling me who I was and how I fitted into this vast mosaic called life.

She would make roti and bakes and go to share it with the

Indian lady who lived all alone in the big house on King Street. The two of them would sit there in the shade drinking lemonade and chit-chatting in their sing-song voice all afternoon, while I fell asleep on the hammock in the backyard.

I spent over three years in New Amsterdam, resenting my parents at first and after a while seeing the wisdom of their decision. I grew to love the life. In Berbice, I was not afraid of who I was and who I was to become. I could just let the life flow allow me to emerge as I was.

The cool breeze calmed my brain. I found I could focus, and Granny just did not let up. She made sure I concentrated on the right things. Did not tell her about the girls chasing the pretty boy, as they called me. Certainly, did not tell her about losing my virginity to Elizabeth, the girl with the long flowing Indian hair and pretty mouth, who had given me the "look" the first morning I arrived at school.

There was no need to tell her about the progress I was making with my studies. No, that news was always ahead of me. Each day I came home I would be told, "Oh I heard you got 100 per cent in your maths revision today, by the way how come you only got 90 per cent in your literature, and it was Chaucer who wrote The Canterbury Tales."

She pushed, cajoled, and nurtured me in the gentlest of ways and created the environment in her house, where I wanted to please her by doing good. And doing good, I did.

I came back to England in the spring of 1980, determined to fight the injustices I saw in the white world.

And what do I do? I fall in love with a white woman.

CHAPTER

FIVE

WHEN I ARRIVED BACK AT Heathrow Airport with eight O-Levels and three A-levels and an offer to go to University College London, (UCL), dad looked at me and smiled. I cut my eye at him but then grinned back to say "Alright, Alright, I get the message." We laughed, hugged each other, and went back to the house in Clapton.

In that summer of 1980, I grew closer to my siblings, my confidence in myself increased, and I found the younger ones were now coming to me for advice about every little thing. Mother used to give me a sneaky look of what I can only describe as admiration and pride when she thought I was not looking. Little did she know I was always watching, for I loved her so much.

I remember all the battles she had to fight for me, her refusal to take rejections from public officials and teachers as she tried to get the best for her new baby, her firstborn in a cold, unloving place.

In October 1980, I was off to Uni to study Economics at UCL, little realising that I would be the only black person in my class. I had been almost four years in Guyana being myself in a mixed society, where your colour just did not come up in the significant way it seemed to permeate everything in England. Here, I was once again trying to make connections with other students a year younger than me and failing.

I was in one of the coffee shops, "Alone Again" as Gilbert O'Sullivan would say, when this peach of a girl came waltzing in. I say peach because her complexion was fresh, her hair was blonde in a battle with ginger, and with blonde winning slightly. It was her eyes, however, that transfixed you. They held you in their gaze and commanded you to look into them.

They were aquamarine, sometimes light blue, at other times (as I found out later) depending on her mood, the darkest of blues. But when she was happy, they were the gentlest of the blues. They seemed to caress you. They made you feel like she would always be there for you. Like you were the only person in her universe.

She came in, surrounded by a large group of admirers, but she was taking no notice of them, the way a lady ignores her minions. All the boys were fighting to see who would buy her coffee, and she seemed tired of them all.

I looked up to see what all the commotion was, and our

eyes met. A sudden charge went through my body, but I decided white girls were not on my menu and went back, head down to my studies.

I felt her taking quick peeps at me when she thought neither I nor anyone else was looking, and one of those times I expected her move and looked straight into her blue eyes when she was not expecting it. We looked at each other for what seemed an eternity before I looked down and continued my work. After a short while, she left alone.

The next day, I started wondering if this girl was hunting me down. As I turned into Lansdowne Terrace, from Guilford Street, on my way to visit a friend in International Hall, I saw her waiting outside the main entrance. She was looking up and down the street as if she was waiting for someone and became relaxed when she saw me. Almost as if she knew I would come down that road.

She smiled when she saw me and acted surprised that I was outside International Hall. I told her I was going to see a friend in the Hall.

"So, what are you studying?" she asked. I told her.

"Fresher, I take it?" she continued, following me as I made my way up the stairs, passing security, into the lobby.

"Yeah," I said, "I am in the first year."

She noticed that the time spent in Guyana had left me with a bit of an accent, and she looked at me, saying:

"I am in the first year, too. By the way, where are you from?"

"'Hackney," I replied. But I knew what she meant.

The next day, I was just about to enter Russell Square

Underground Station, when I saw the girl with the deep blue eyes running towards the station as if she is in a hurry. I smiled at her as she caught up with me and we made our way down to the trains.

I went to Platform One, heading towards Manor House, and she went in the opposite direction towards Uxbridge. As we went our different ways, I took a sneaky look back at her. Short black leather jacket, a denim mini skirt displaying legs to the top of her thighs, and a scarf that just followed her. Blonde hair bouncing as if it had a life of its own.

We kept bumping into each other throughout the week. There must have been thousands of students at UCL, but our paths just kept crossing. On a Sunday morning, as I was making my way towards Euston Station, I saw her coming towards me as she turned left onto Gower Street from Euston Road.

She looked as if she had been out all night and was crawling back to get some rest.

She smiled and said something like: "We can't go on bumping into each other like this. I think it must mean something."

"What do you think it means?" I said.

"I don't know," she came back, "but I think we owe it to ourselves to find out, don't you?"

"How do we go about that?" I asked.

"Well, you could ask me out and see what I say."

"Where would you want to go?" I teased.

"You're asking me out. You suggest," she said impatiently.

Then she seemed to remember something and said: "Ah, I know. I've got a couple of tickets to see Evita, the Tim Rice, and

Andrew Lloyd Webber musical about Eva Peron, for Saturday. Supposed to take my friend out as a treat for her birthday, but she won't mind. Not sure she is all that keen on musicals, anyway, doesn't enjoy being indoors, would rather gallop away over the Downs on her horse. Shall we go to that?"

"You're asking me out?" I teased again.

She looked at me in a deep and thoughtful way, and I swear her eyes were no longer dark blue, they became light blue and easy as she said, "Yes."

We agreed to meet at 6:30 p.m. outside the Prince Edward Theatre on Old Compton Street, where the musical was showing. I said, "Take care." She said, "Ciao," and we went off on our separate journeys.

It was the first time I had been to any theatre. Wasn't somewhere I went, no history of it. The last four years in Guyana meant that the cinema was a place I went to when I went to Georgetown, as the projector in New Amsterdam had broken down and no one could get a repair or replacement for it.

The theatre was an unfamiliar experience for me, and I fell in love with Eva Peron and wanted to be Che, who bore a striking resemblance to that iconic photo of Che Guevara. David Essex was cool, and he played Che as someone who was going to change the world if he did not die first.

The girl with the dark blue eyes sat there listening to Peron's mistress sing "Another Suitcase In Another Hall" and then I saw her eyes glisten and become lost in awe and wonder as Elaine Paige sang "Don't Cry For Me Argentina". She was a little girl lost in the song's magic. The tune was about an event she did not understand, but it filled her right to the brim at that precise moment. She was in Argentina. She was Eva Peron.

Out of the corner of my eye, I saw her eyes reflect the beam from one of the stage lights. I saw her face internalise every emotion that was going on in the singer's voice, in the singer's actions, in the singer's face. She made me feel she needed to be protected from a cruel world, that she could not withstand the pressures that this world offered. And something deep inside of me made me want to hide her from the pain, to protect her from the delicacy of her own being.

Her innocence and gentleness of soul, at that moment so overwhelmed me, I have been in love with her ever since.

I came out of that theatre on Old Compton Street in love with the theatre and in love with your mum.

We walked back to her lodgings in Russell Square, and she just kept talking. She spoke about her life growing up in Chichester, her weekends in Worthing and her mum and dad.

She told me about her family over coffee in Old Compton Street, her love of London, how she loved the busyness of the city, how it gave her a charge–and the people, "Wow, the people!" she cried. The different people you saw every day. It was not like that in Sussex, where you just saw the same faces all the time, you had the same conversation repeatedly, and there were never any countervailing views. Everyone thought the same. Opinions never differed, so after a while, everyone felt the same way about everything.

In London, there was a counter-argument for every thought under the sun. There were Muslim doctors, Rasta engineers,

Polish accountants, and Jewish builders living alongside the native English people, and no one seemed to notice. Everyone had a different view of the world, and she enjoyed the freedom that brought.

I had never thought about it that way, but then I had been away for over three years and was just getting used to the place again, besides I had never travelled out of Hackney much, no need to. Had everyone and everything I needed around me.

I did not get a word in back to Russell Square. She wanted to tell me who she'd been, who she was, and who she was going to be. I allowed all her dreams to flood out. I knew the world she summoned was one I wanted to share–and although life had made me far too cynical for my years; I bought into her dream. I also believed that it was possible. You just had to want it enough.

Your mum's and my expression of our love are between your mum and me. I am from an age where I would find it difficult to share that with my children. But let me say this once: your mum, and I loved each other, and she is the woman for whom I would have given my life. She will always be.

Anyway, as I was saying, I loved your mum, and I think your mother fell in love with the idea of me. I mean, she did not know me, she could not envisage what falling in love with me was going to be like.

Not that I was an evil man, or she was an unruly woman or anything like that. We just underestimated the effects of the insular attitudes of an island race, with a warlike men-tality on naïve young people in love. But I should have known better. I should not have forgotten in those moments of total besottedness, what my mother had drummed into me about being an outsider in England.

I thought that being half-white entitled me to at least half of whatever privileges that came with being English, white or British. Kids, I was so wrong.

Your mother hid me from her family for almost three years, and all the time she became a virtual lodger in my home. She got to know all my family, my brother, and sister, my dad, and my mum, your grandmother.

Now and then, she would go home to Sussex and would come back early Sunday evening, almost as if she could not wait to get back to our house, where she felt at home. Her family was always away, or busy whenever I suggested meeting them, and I just let it go.

At last, I met them at the graduation ceremony in late July 1983, when I was introduced as a friend along with all her other pals. I was about to have a chat with her mother when your mum diverted the conversation and steered her mother away to meet some other friends. Her mum turned back and gave me the deepest of looks. I smiled and turned so she could not see into my eyes.

We carried on like this for about another 18 months, until my mum said to me one day in the deep Irish twang she used when she was upset, "Is that bloody girl ever going to let her parents know she is going out with a black man, or is she going to hide you from them forever?"

"Do you think she is ashamed of me or something, Mum?" I asked.

"She seemed so confident about everything. I cannot see her being ashamed of me, Mum," I said, whilst in my mind, I was retracing every conversation, decisions, journeys we had ever made and realised that there may be something in what my mum was saying.

Your mum once said to me she'd never thought about racism or even "coloured" people until she met me. She saw people of a different hue when she first came to London, but most of them seemed to be busy living their lives and they did not interact with her much.

Her crowd was primarily white British with a few Jewish girls who went to the London unis'. They were the people she hung around with. Now and then she would go to a party in Ladbroke Grove or Paddington and would dance with a coloured guy and would be asked questions by her girlfriends about what it was like, as if she had done something exotic and daring.

One Saturday night she had gone to the 'Q' club with a guy who had a lot of black friends and had enjoyed the music and the atmosphere. But she had never gone back. In London she felt free, not controlled by the inhibitions of Sussex.

One day, through heaving sobs, she told me that two years earlier on a Bank Holiday weekend, a few months after she had met me, she and her mum had been walking through Chichester. She was about to tell her mum that she had met this nice coloured boy, and she liked him when a black man came around the corner towards them.

She had never seen a black man in Chichester before, and

she smiled at him. Her mother was furious, saying: "Why are you smiling at that nigger, do you know him? Hope you are not hanging around with any of that sort in London, sweetheart. God, that would break our hearts."

Her words died in her mouth. "Course not, Mum," she lied. "As if I could do such a thing."

I remembered her crying that Sunday as she said that she felt as if she had betrayed me, and wondering whether when push comes to shove, she would always betray me.

After that conversation about the incident in Chichester, she stopped seeing me for a couple of weeks and I was so busy with exams and stuff that I did not even notice, until my Mum said one day, "Where is that girl of yours? Are you two still see-ing each other?" I think she hoped I would say, "No, I am seeing a black girl now." That would have made her feel more at ease.

"I am busy right now, Mum. Ain't got time for girls, too many exams and tests."

She gazed at me, then made some rotis. I used to smile when I saw my Irish mum trying to make rotis. I mean they weren't too bad, but I had been eating rotis made by my granny in Guyana for three years, and they were the best rotis I had ever tasted in my life. Even now, after forty years, I can still remem-ber the taste as the spices hit the back of my throat, on the way down to my stomach.

The Monday after that chat with mum, I was standing outside her lecture hall (yeah, I know, I was weak) waiting and getting the usual looks from people who were wondering what I was doing there.

She saw me first and turned around to go back inside the hall, but something made her swivel back around, and our eyes met. I smiled at her and moved my head from one side to the other as a gesture to say, "I see you, please come here." She joined me, and we walked in silence down to the British Museum.

We talked, and she asked me how I had been, said she had been going home at the weekend, as her dad wasn't feeling too well and she was also wondering if I could go out with someone who had such a racist family.

She was sincere in that conversation, you know, guys. Said she was not sure that the way her family hated coloured people wouldn't rub off on her. It petrified her that their habits would become hers, and she did not know what that meant for her future.

Now I have had a long time to reflect on the signs, the little things I noticed but did not think about too much. I realise now that your mother never recovered from the treatments her parents, especially her mother, doled out in trying to convince her to abandon me and run back to the safety of a lovely white boy from Sussex or Surrey, or even from up North.

The phone calls, the taunts, the "nigger lover" tirades that would have come down the phone like a storm every time she phoned home, the caustic comments, isolation, and alienation, yet she still refused to give me up.

And I, in my innocence, knew nothing of the war that raged in her young life. She kept it all hidden behind the smile she had for me, the laugh, her laidback, relaxed behaviour when she was with my mum and dad.

Had I known any of this, I would have let her go. I would not have watched her having to choose between her family and me. I would have allowed her to find that white boy from Sussex, Surrey, or even up North because by now I loved her very much. Enough to put her first.

I graduated with a first from UCL, bought some proper clothes and got a job with one of your competitors as a Trainee Management Consultant. My God, those days were busy; it was like I was an apprentice, following the consultants around like sheep following a shepherd. One month I was in Germany working as a note-taker in a large motor manufacturer, next month in Italy working out the price of wines.

I was so busy those days. I only snatched a few days with your mum between assignments and on the odd occasions, she would come and have a few days with me wherever I was.

Your mum always wanted to be an artist. She would get lost in the potential, the possibilities. I would be focused on the present, the here and now. I only ever saw what was in front of me. One and one was only ever going to make two in my universe. Your mum would try to make them become as many things as she could.

She did a charcoal drawing of me that brought parts of me to visibility that I had never been aware of before. Her insight was so intuitive. Her pencil almost penetrated my soul. I swear that every time I see that drawing; I notice something else. You know the drawing I am talking about.

I am on a veranda in Spain looking into the room and she

is looking at me from inside the room. When I see that picture, I remember every detail of that day. Your mum could have been a celebrated artist, but somehow, she did not have the discipline to work every day. She would wait until she was inspired to work, and she was not inspired very often.

I always felt she could have achieved more had she wanted to. This hidden thought of mine, this intuition, would find expression as we settled down to establish a home and a family.

But I am getting ahead of myself.

When she told her family that I had proposed and she had accepted, they abandoned her. She cried all night, and her eyes stayed dark blue for four days. My fiery Irish mother, who remembered her own past held her tight and squeezed some hope back into her.

We got married in the summer of 1986, a year after they promoted me to a permanent consultant. We bought the house on Bressey Grove in South Woodford, close enough to the school–and the underground station for me to get to work. Your mum was not all that interested in finding permanent employment. She did not seem to have the drive to take full advantage of her degree. Looking back now, I wonder if the issues with her family about me had left her in a state of permanent depression. Was this the price she paid for loving me?

Our wedding was quiet, registry office style. No sign of her mum, her dad, or any of her family. There were my mum and dad, three of her friends and two of mine from Uni, and my brother and sister. We went for a lovely meal in a fancy French restaurant in George Lane, by the station and a week's honeymoon in Cascais near Lisbon in Portugal. That was the start of our life together.

It took two years to do up the house in Bressy Grove, and those two years in that house were the happiest of my life. All I did was mow the lawn on a Saturday morning, and your mum did the rest.

She decorated the house from top to bottom, got builders in to alter it, fitting a new kitchen and bathrooms, and landscaped the garden. She painted every room, fitted all tiles and grouted them. I tell you some of her ideas were so creative. I used to look at her in awe. She used to show me a masterpiece and just say, "What do you think?" as I stood there with my mouth wide open.

We, I think I should say she finished the house two months before you were born, twenty-nine years ago. I felt we were happy, but sometimes I would see her trying to phone someone and as soon as she said "It's me", she would have to redial, which sounded to me like the other person was putting the phone down on her. It felt as if she was waging a private war with the person on the other end of the line, trying to force them to talk to her. They never did. Then she would place the receiver down and go to the toilet where she would stay for ages.

I guessed she was trying to let her mum know she was a mother herself, to tell her about the baby and herself, perhaps to hint that a visit would be welcomed. To show how well her life was turning out.

Her mum would not forgive her for marrying some "half-caste" boy.

Do you remember your grandad, son? He died in Guyana, and Mum and I had to bring him back. My mum came to live with us part of the week after his death, and my mum and your mum were at war with each other.

Looking back now, I think I understand. My mum resented Dad dying and leaving her all alone in England. She would have loved to have gone back to Glendalough in Ireland to spend her last days, but there was no one left there for her to go back to. The rest of her life was going to be in England, a place she had never grown to love because, in her mind, it had never loved her.

Your mum's resentment and fear came from a feeling that what happened to my mum was how she would end up as well. Abandoned in a place she did not know and cut off from the people who mattered the most to her. Whatever it was, they fought like cats and dogs, and it only eased up when your sister was born. Sis, it seemed like you gave them both something to take their minds off their perceived future and a reason to love the present.

My mum died in 1996, a hot Sunday in July. Feeling tired, she had gone upstairs to lie down. I called her for supper, and she did not answer. Thinking she was in a deep sleep, I went up to wake her and saw that the slumber was so much deeper than I had expected. We buried her on top of my dad in Manor Park cemetery. My brother, my sister and I became close again, just like we did when Dad died, but as the months went by, the visits became less and less until all we have left are the obligatory phone calls on birthdays and Christmas.

Sadly, you know kids, the racism and all the other indignities that we children of the '60s and '70s went through have made us insensitive. We got so used to being called "Wog", "Coon", "Jungle Bunny" and all the other terms, we forget how painful it must be when you do not expect it, to be called "Nigger Lover" or "Wog Bait" by your own so-called people.

Because the experiences have turned our feelings to stone, we cannot see how a white girl you are going out with or married to could be made insane by those words.

For her, it meant she had been discarded, abandoned, kicked out by her own people. She had to rely on a different tribe for her survival and her esteem. It was even more traumatic when she remembered her tribe has always thought of her new tribe as inferior, worthless savages.

I'm not sure when I realised your mum resented me, kinda wished I was someone or something else. It may have been a growing awareness, a quiet glance she may have given a man, a shy downturn of the head and a smile to herself, then a look at me with those dark blue eyes, that never seem to leave her after you were born Sis, and my mother died.

Again, because I have had a lot of time to think about it all, I think your mum's eyes looked at everything and saw nothing she liked. It sometimes felt that I was mourning for my mum and your mum was grieving for her old life. The life of certainty, where everything made sense, and people looked up at and to her, instead of the double-takes, the snide comments, the disrespect she had to endure walking up to the school, taking you kids' out on the Drive, or popping into Marks & Spencer.

She never wanted to be some display mannequin, someone on permanent display, but that is how she would have still felt after ten years in the quiet, upmarket village-cum-town of South Woodford.

After all these years, I still don't know if it was all in her mind. That haunts me. Was it that your mum expected it, therefore saw a hatred, a contempt that was not there?

Was she so filled with the longing to find peace with her family that she was blaming everyone in South Woodford for her situation? I still don't know.

I mean I have never had a lot of issues with the people there; we talked superficial stuff in the supermarkets, football in the pub, and about our kids on the rare occasions I picked you guys up from school. So, in all honesty, South Woodford was not as bad as Hackney was when I was going to school. But that could have been because by then I was immune to the insults.

It was about 4:00 pm on Thursday, 25 June 1998 when I received a phone call from the headteacher at your school to say your mum had not picked you both up.

I rang home immediately. No answer. I rang the head-teacher back to see if your mum had picked you two up while I was on the phone trying to ring mum. The slightly annoyed voice on the other end told me the answer was no. I apologised profusely. Told the voice I was on my way.

After deliberation, I decided that the Central Line was the quickest way to get home, so I ran down to Bank station and tried ringing your mum until I could not get any mobile phone signal underground. I started trying to ring her again when I got to Stratford. Still no answer. After six rings the answerphone came on with the by now familiar message about sorry, but tied up right now, leave a message, will call you back later. Her voice sounded so warm, so close, I imagined she was home, messing me about.

I got out of South Woodford station, ran up George Lane, then turned right on Woodford Road, past Gates the car retailer and into Churchfields, where the headteacher is by the gate, and you are both clinging onto each other as if your world has just ended and looking confused. But as you know kids, that was the start of our bewilderment.

None of us uttered a word as we walked for what seemed an eternity down the High Road, turning right into Bressy Grove and along the pavement to our house. I turned the key, and the three of us walked in.

Sis, you shouted "Mum" and ran into the kitchen, came running back out, saying "She is not there, must be upstairs. Mum?" you said, scampering up the stairs. "Mum!" Sis, you called again; voice more desperate than before. You ran down the stairs and into the garden saying, "She is not up there, Dad."

Son, you looked at me almost as if you knew what was going on, almost as if the thing you prayed would not happen had occurred and you had been powerless to stop it. You said nothing; you put down your satchel and went out into the garden to hold your sister and squeezed her to protect her from the very thing you were afraid of. You knew your mum was not coming back. That she had gone. I do not know how you knew what it was in her behaviour that had sown those seeds of doubt and fear in you, but you knew.

I often wondered over the years about that, you know kids, was your mum showing you she was not coping and I, too blind, too busy, too trusting to see that, allowed her to plant undesirable doubts, fears and trepidation into your tiny little soul? Did you both pick up those signals that I was too blind to see or feel?

I went over to the telephone table in the hall to ring your mum's friend from keep-fit and put the phone back on its hook, because lying there was an envelope with your mum's writing on it.

I sat on the chair beside the table, used my index finger to open the envelope, and this is what the letter said. It is funny, after 19 years I still walk around with it like it is some great talisman that I must never let out of my sight. Something that reminds me of who and what I am dealing with and the power of hate.

The letter was not long, not what you would expect from someone who was destroying so many lives. It was heavy on brevity. Very matter-of-fact. Like someone who was writing it in a hurry. Someone who wanted to say something because it needed to be said, but wanted to get out in a hurry, before someone came and forced them to change their mind.

She did not want anyone to reason her out of the corner she had painted herself in. She was a bolter, and she was going to bolt.

As you must remember Son, having read it all those years ago. This is what your mother had written.

Hello Love,

I am sorry, sorry, sorry, sorry, so sorry, but I cannot take this life anymore. It is killing me day by day, week after week, year after year, and although I love you and the kids more than myself, I cannot take it anymore.

I am lost in a sea of unfriendly, hate-filled faces. Alone, so alone. Cut off from everything and everyone I knew.

I know that my mum and dad's family would rather die than accept you and the kids as part of their family, and since I cannot live without them, I only have one choice. To stay with you and the kids would make me resent you all more and more until I think I would hate you. And I will not allow that.

I know what I am doing is unforgivable, so I am not even going to ask for forgiveness. Tell the kids I will always love them if you can bring yourself to do so.

Don't come looking for me. I have decided.

I am gone.

I never saw your mum, my wife, my friend (so I thought) again. My certainty that this was all some joke started fading pretty much straight away. I searched and found her mum's phone number and rang it. The phone was picked up: no answer.

I said, "Hello?" They put the phone down. When I rang again, they did not answer the phone.

I rang friends: "Have you heard anything?"

"No," said all her friends, "but if I hear anything, I'll call you back."

No one ever did for nearly three years.

My beautiful Sis, you cried yourself to sleep most nights, woke up in the morning drowning in urine. Bedclothes changed daily, Dettol smell from your room until you were twelve years old.

Son, the middle distance was your favourite place for a long, long time. That is where you lived, staring into the middle distance with a vacant smile to protect you from yourself and everyone else.

My dad's mum had taught me well in those years in Guyana. No one was ever going to destroy me or anything that I loved again. I swore on my grandmother's memory that we would get through this and that whatever life thought it had in store for us, we would get through this.

The first contact with your mother after she walked out was two years later when I received papers requesting a divorce. After running them through with my solicitor, I signed them and sent them back, keeping a copy of course. She said she wanted nothing from me, which was just as well because she was getting nothing. All she could ever get from me was my love, and that was not wanted.

Both of you had been holding out for the reconciliation, and I could see the hope dying in both of your faces when I told *you that your mum wanted a divorce. I remember you saying, "Doesn't she want us anymore, Dad?"*

Even after two years, your hope had not died. Still, the umbilical cord that held you to your mother was intact, still coloured how you viewed the world.

I replied, "Mum is going through troublesome times, you know guys." But I cried that night as your words ravaged my thoughts, and I could find nothing constructive to say to either of you.

The greatest pain I suffered during those years after your mother abandoned us was watching both your faith and trust in people become emaciated and fragile. I watched as you sought assurances from me for the smallest things, "What time you coming back, Dad?" was the most frequently asked question from both of you.

Within six months of the divorce becoming final, a friend of ours that I had not heard from in three years rang to say that your mum was getting married again and that a baby was on the way. I heard another baby followed eighteen months later. Your mum now also had a white family, and you had white half-siblings. A family of people we did not know.

I remembered smiling when I heard all that. Your mum had got what she had always wanted, what she should have gone for in the first place, and leave me and mine alone. But I wondered whether it gave the friend satisfaction to tell me this, or was it some kind of civic duty?

From that day on, I swear that my heart became a thing of stone. I have never fallen in love again and although there have been love affairs. No, not love affairs. Not the real thing that pulverises the heart and takes your breath away, that makes you anxious waiting for something coming that will overwhelm you. No, I have had none of those, perhaps because I chose not to have any. These affairs were more events created by necessity, a need for a warm embrace on a cold winter night, so to speak.

None of them took place at my house, our home. They happened in other countries, other towns, other dwellings. My home became a place of celibacy.

My life became one of making sure that my children did not fail in anything. I used the clock, the processes, the systems to ensure that both of you would always come out near the top in everything you tried. I watched the two of you grow from the lost, abandoned children of that night into the capable people you are today.

And when I look at you, I feel encouraged by the decisions I made, but deep down I ask myself, always, did I do the right thing?

Perhaps all she wanted was for me to come and get her, to show that I would die for her, to let her know she meant so much to me and together we could withstand anything. I will never ever know.

What I know is that it has left me crippled by the experience, and I will never fall in love again.

CHAPTER

SIX

LAST CHAPTER
2017

I FINISHED READING DAD'S EMAIL attachment about two o'clock in the morning, turned the laptop off and tried to get some of that sleep I had promised myself, but Dad's words kept coming back to me forcing me to revisit things and times that I thought were gathering a little dust. I knew I did not want to ruffle the "Do Not Disturb" signs I had placed all around them. Not again.

I thought of Sis and opened the laptop again and fired off an email to her to say Dad had written a lot of stuff about when Mum left and to read them when she not too busy, or occupied.

I knew for me, there would be no sleep that night as the pain would come back, that sense of guilt and loss would plague me until I could get it back under control.

I did not want to remember any of this. I had spent my life since Mum left trying to prevent my imagination from summoning her, from seeing her giving Sis bits of bread to feed the ducks in Eagle Pond, from sensing what she was doing at each hour point of the day. From seeing those aquamarine eyes that shone so brightly when she was positive turn to the darkest blue as she picked up another signal that she had let someone down in her society, her community–no, her tribe. The tribe that my sister, my dad and I were not a part of.

Why now, Dad? Why, when I am understanding your motivation, do you bring uncertainties into my thought processes?

What can I do with uncertainties? I cannot act on them. They just leave me frozen, unable to move forward or backwards. They leave me impotent, and I will never again be impotent. I will never again allow failure to so overwhelm me it takes all of my confidence. Never.

And I never want to go back to that afternoon on which our mother abandoned us and put insecurity into our psyche.

My sister and I blamed ourselves for Mum abandoning us on Thursday, 25 June 1998, at 3:30 p.m.

Should have seen it coming. We knew something was wrong. We, too, had felt those eyes on us as we walked up Woodford Road, as we ran down George Lane to Marks &

Spencer. As for those people at the posh end of the Drive, well let's not even go there.

I often wonder if we'd have been better off being brought up in Hackney, where more people looked like us. We could see Mum wilting, but she had trained us not to betray her by telling Dad about our concerns. She made Dad out to be the enemy, and we believed her.

I was ten years old, coming up eleven, last year in Junior School and taking exams to get to Forest Private School and the 11 plus, to get into Ilford County Grammar School.

I was studying and taking extra private lessons to get to Forest School, as it was within walking distance from our home. Ilford County was OK, but not as nice as Forest, was my ten-year-old opinion.

Sis was in the second year of primary school and was smarter than me in many ways.

We were an excellent team together, Sis and I. Although she was five years younger, she would ask me profound questions that always started with the word "Why?" She got so good that I used to dread that "Why?"

I knew my mum. I was the centre of her attention from the time I was born until Sis came along. My observation of her, her moods, her chitter-chatter, her laughs, her melancholy would only cease when Dad came home and played with me for an hour. Then Mum would take me to bed and read long stories while Dad busied himself with his dinner and letters. So, until Sis came along, I had Mum all to myself. In the end, I could feel her rhythms, both negative and positive.

It eased up a bit when I went into reception class and when Sis was born four months later, but by then I knew my mum very well.

Thursday, 25 June 1998 was a peculiar day, perhaps the most memorable day of my life. Even until now. I remember every action. Every word said by everyone, every moment like it was a film. It overshadows me, getting my first-class degree from King's, my first kiss, my first holiday, everything.

Dad had left for work as usual by the time my eyes opened and my nose smelt the onions, garlic, and thyme going into the bottom of the frying pan to make the scrambled eggs with bacon bits that Mum so loved to prepare for breakfast on those special occasions. This treat was usually for birthdays and the Christmas and Easter holidays. Bran Flakes or Shredded Wheat would often be the order of the day as we rushed between getting washed, cleaning our teeth, putting on our school uniform and getting out the house in time to be two minutes late for school. But this morning, Mum looked as if she had been up for a long time. I asked her whose birthday it was; she looked at me, smiled and said: "This is because I love you guys and just wanted you to know that."

I looked at her quizzically, but at the time did not understand what she meant. Of course, I knew my mum loved me. All mums and dads loved their kids, didn't they?

She spent ages moisturising my face and arms, and as for Sis's hair, well it took so long Sis nearly had a fit, but Mum wouldn't or couldn't stop caressing us. It was embarrassing.

Ordinarily, she would let us run ahead of her up Woodford

Road, shouting "Stop" if we went too far ahead. Not that morning. That morning she held our hands so tightly that even Sis wanted to squirm out of her grip and run all the way past Gates, the car shop, past the library and then into school.

That miserable June morning it rained all the way to school. But Mum did not notice the rain and the cold. She came out in a thin cardigan and forgot the umbrella, even though it was pelting down. Sis and I had our hoods up on our rain jackets. Mum was strolling as if she had forgotten that this was the rainiest and coldest June for years.

I asked her why she was crying as she released our hands in the school playground, and she said that a fly had gone into her eye. She wiped her eyes, shook her head as if clearing out some unwelcome thought and said: "Love you guys, Mummy will always love you."

We both said, "Yeah, yeah, we know, Mum," as we both ran away from her clutches into the queues that were forming to get into our classes.

Course she loves us, we thought confidently. All mothers love their kids.

It did not totally surprise me when Mum did not pick us up on Thursday, 25 June 1998, at 3:30 pm.

All the inconsistencies that I had noticed in Mum's behaviour that morning now made sense to me, her empathic, intuitive, and sensitive ten-year-old son.

I remembered the day my mum tried to run away from me in George Lane, that time when the old lady called her "bloody coon lover" and my worst fears started overtaking my thoughts. My mum had gone, and we would never see her again. That entered my head at 3:35 pm, on Thursday, 25 June 1998.

I started staring off into the middle distance at 4 pm five minutes after the headteacher called us into her office to say that Mum had not turned up and she was going to contact our dad to pick us up. Did we know his mobile number to save her looking it up? I gave it to her and continued staring until Dad came and took us on that fast but taking-forever walk home.

I was looking trance like into the middle distance as Dad turned the deadbolt key, then the Yale to open the front door, and Sis ran inside and shouted, "Mum!" The house never answered back, it just stood there, silent, unbreathing, still. All that could be heard was the pitter-patter of tiny raindrops as they made their way down the gutter to remind us that the rain was not yet ready to give up and was going to continue for a long time.

I looked at Dad, trying to see if he had any notion of what was going on. He was in a state of total bewilderment. Meanwhile, action woman Sis had run upstairs, shouting, "Mum, where are you? We are home." Again, the patter of raindrops was the world's only response.

Sis ran down the stairs saying in a now-desperate, fearful voice, no longer a sound filled with surprise, now a cry of shock, "SHE IS NOT UP THERE, DAD. WHERE IS SHE!!?" As she rushed to the back door, turned and grabbed the key off the shelf and opened the door, shouting, "Mum!" in what I could only describe as a voice of victory. After all, where else could she be? Even with the rain pelting down, Sis thought Mum must be outside. After all, where else could she be?

Sis ran into the garden and to the shed, while the rain lashed at her hair, looked in the rabbit hutch. No sign of Mum. My sister ran over to the giant oak tree where Mum would usually sit and plait her hair. Not there. Glanced up at the damsons still waiting to ripen in the faint hope Mum might be playing a very serious game of hide and seek. But Mum was nowhere to be found. She was not there, anywhere, nowhere.

Sis let out the most profound scream of pain I have ever heard and groaned as Dad picked her up and soothed her hair, put his cheek against hers and then kissed her forehead. Sis did not stop crying for the rest of the night.

I remember re-reading the letter again Dad had shown me earlier, almost reluctantly. Dad then whispered to me, when Sis had gone to bed, that it looked like Mum had gone to stay with her mum and dad. And he was not sure when–or if–she was coming back.

I never cried. I wish I had. But I would never cry.

If Mum could do this to Sis, to me, to Dad, she just was not worth my tears. She had obviously never loved us, or she could not do this. I will never love someone who does not love me and welcomed the anaesthesia of the trance-like stare into the middle distance. It soothed and comforted me. It allowed me to walk through the valley of the shadows, unharmed, unmoved by all that chaos around me.

Dad said he was going to look after us the way his grandmother in New Amsterdam would have done; that his

"Granny", as he called her, would have done this, would have said that.

> Dad showed us tough love
> Kind-hearted love
> Love full of wisdom
> Fulfilling love
> Love with no conditions
> He expected nothing back

And it devoted us to him. We may not have always shown him how much we cared, but we both knew that he made us strong, and we would both die for him.

But the lady with the aquamarine and ever-changing eyes still haunts my sleep, and I think of her most nights. I think I will always miss my mum.

And Sis, my beautiful Sis with the hazel eyes that go darker when she is troubled, is on the television picking up another award for her acting talent. She is the foremost young acting talent in England, a year after leaving RADA and five years after leaving Forest School, where we both ended up.

She does not wet the bed anymore and cries so easily for someone who is as hard as a diamond. You just would not want to go up against her. She is formidable.

She gets so lost in her roles; they say she becomes the characters she plays.

But then, Sis never found herself again.

Not after the night of Thursday, 25 June 1998.

POSTSCRIPT

MY FATHER SAID TO ME once that he did not know Mum was describing their life together so badly in those early years before she fled.

How silent, afraid and alone she must have felt to see her world through the distorted lens she had created for herself.

I think the distorted lens that my mother gave me to see my father through ended up distorting the lens through which I saw myself.

ABOUT THE AUTHOR

 Roy Merchant was born in Jamaica. He left there in 1961 to join his parents in England. He enlisted in the Royal Navy in 1965 and became a submariner, spending most of his submarine years in Singapore, Hong Kong, and other parts of the Far East.

Having left the Navy in 1970, he retrained as an Electronics Engineer, then Technical Manager in a large television rental company in the 1970s.

In the mid-'80s, they recruited him to a senior local government manager post in a London local authority. Retiring in 2014, Roy took a fresh path and started a health and well-being company and dedicating more time to writing and performing poetry across London.

This book is his third, his second is *20 Things I Wish I Knew At 20*, and his first is called, *Walking In The Shadows Of Death*.

Published by:

Relentless Realities
Roy Merchant   Writer and Performance Poet
Website: https://www.relentless-realities.com
Email: roy@relentless-realities.com